Bumpus Jumpus
Dinosaurumpus!

For Maud, Milly and Ben – T.M.

For Sarah, with love – G.P-R.

ORCHARD BOOKS
338 Euston Road, London NW1 3BH
Orchard Books Australia
Level 17/207 Kent Street, Sydney, NSW 2000

First published in 2002 by Orchard Books
First published in paperback in 2003

ISBN 978 1 84121 294 4

A CIP catalogue record for this book is available from the British Library.

20 19 18 17 16 15 14 13 12

Printed in China

Orchard Books is a division of Hachette Children's Books,
an Hachette UK company. www.hachette.co.uk

Bumpus Jumpus Dinosaurumpus!

Tony Mitton

Guy Parker-Rees

ORCHARD

There's a quake and a quiver
and a rumbling around.

It makes you shiver.
It's a thundery sound.

"Shake, shake, shudder...
near the sludgy old swamp.
The dinosaurs are coming.
Get ready to romp.

Watch out for **Deinosuchus** with her **snip-snap** grin, as she perches on her tail and **twizzles** in a spin.

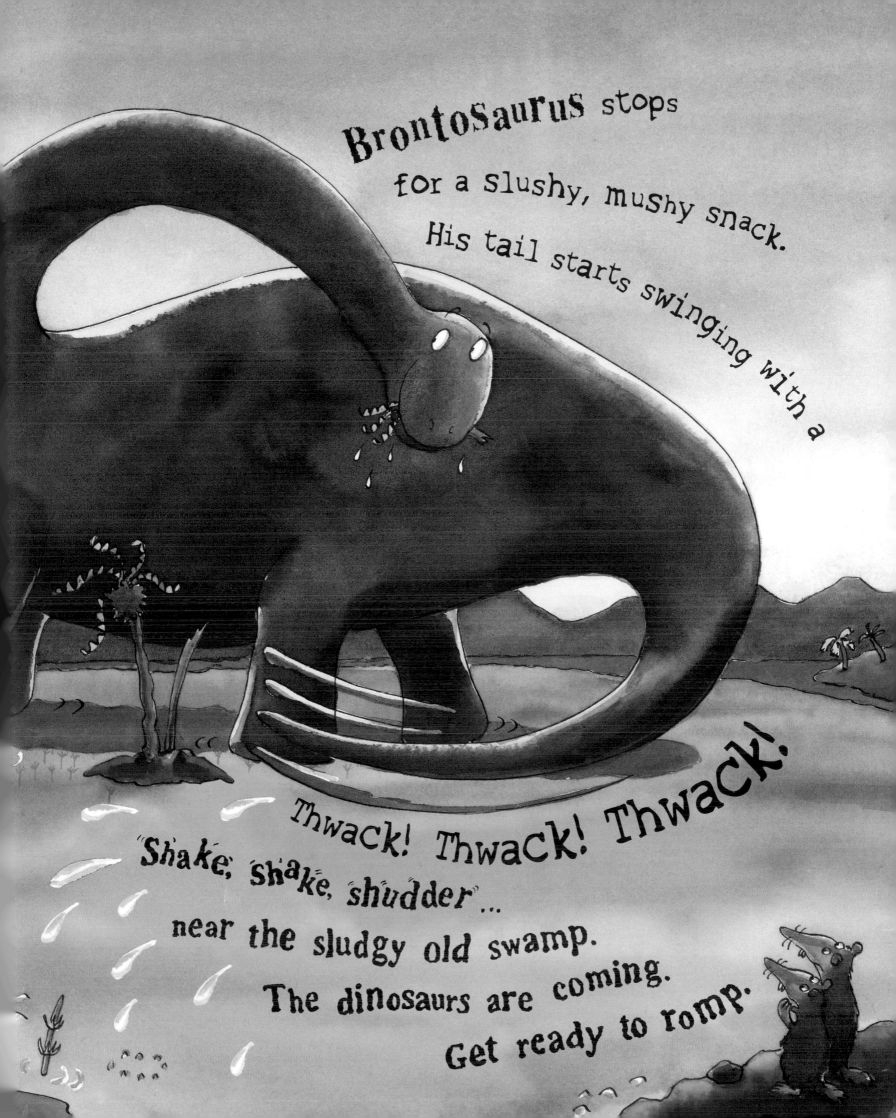

Brontosaurus stops for a slushy, mushy snack.
His tail starts swinging with a

Thwack! Thwack! Thwack!

"Shake, shake, shudder"...
near the sludgy old swamp.
The dinosaurs are coming.
Get ready to romp.

Stegosaurus stomps along with lots of her mates.

Clatter! Clatter! Clatter!

go their bony back plates.

"Shake, shake, shudder"...
near the sludgy old swamp.
The dinosaurs are coming.
Get ready to romp.

Clatter!

Rattle!

Zoom! Zoom!

Come and take a peek...

"Shake, shake, shudder...
near the sludgy old swamp.
Everybody's doing the
dinosaur romp.

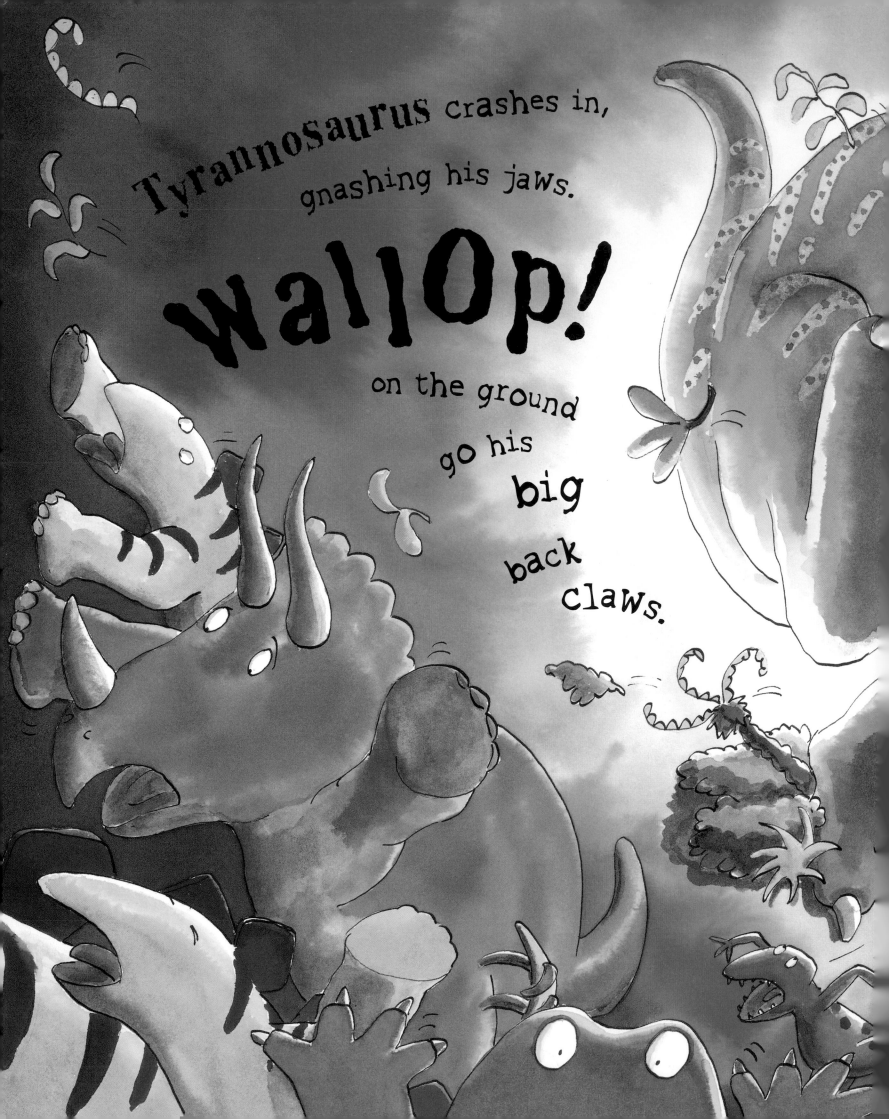

Tyrannosaurus crashes in,
gnashing his jaws.

WallOp!

on the ground
go his
big
back
claws.

He's huge
and he's heavy,
but all he wants to do...

"Shake, shake, shudder...
near the sludgy old swamp.
Everybody's doing the
dinosaur romp.

The dinosaurs won't scratch us,
or bite us, or thump us.
They just want to holler up a...

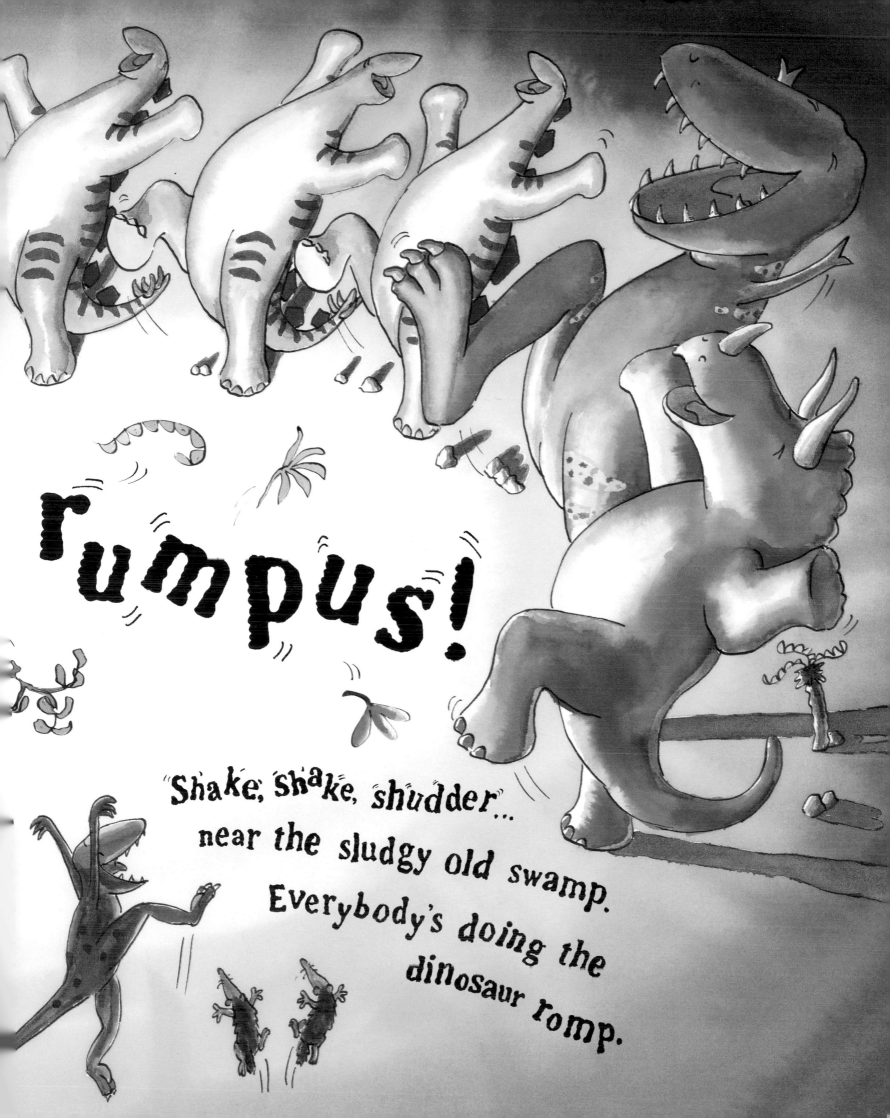

rumpus!

"Shake, shake, shudder...
near the sludgy old swamp.
Everybody's doing the
dinosaur romp.

But soon all the rompers grow sleepy and slow.

till finally the dinosaurs
are all fast asleep.

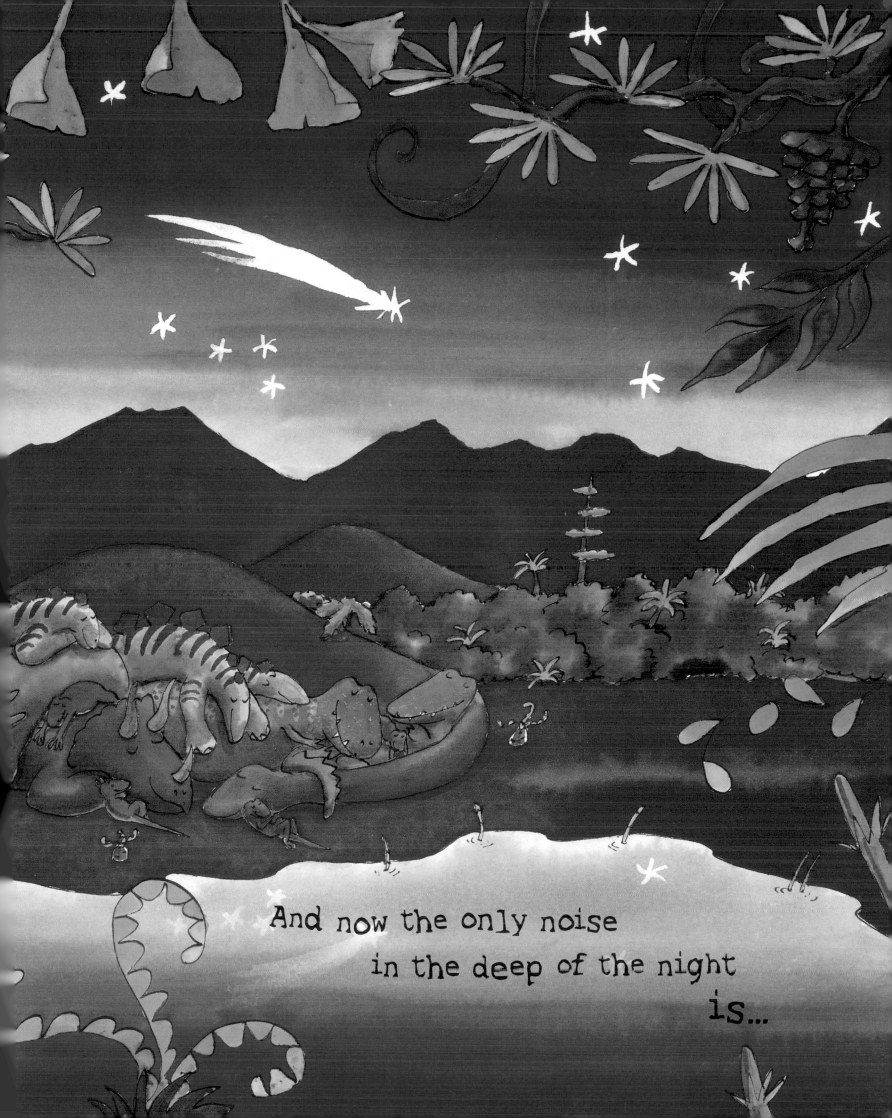

And now the only noise
in the deep of the night
is...

dinosaur-snoring
till the next day's light.